STEP INTO READING

STEP 2

ANNA'S BEST FRIENDS

By Christy Webster

Illustrated by the Disney Storybook Artists

Random House New York

Olaf the snowman

is Anna's friend.

He dreams
of warmer weather.

Reindeer Sven is
Kristoff's friend.

They always
stick together.

A frozen adventure
in a sleigh.

Run, Sven, run!

Get away!

Anna explores

the ice and snow.

Her friends tell her
which way to go.

Anna's sister, Elsa,
makes magical ice.

Sometimes sisters disagree.

Sometimes they are nice.

Sven is brave.
He pulls the sled
higher.

Olaf is brave.

He builds Anna a fire.

Now Anna's adventures
are done.

She and her friends have
some fun!

Elsa, Kristoff,
Olaf, and Sven.

They will always be
Anna's best friends!

Visit us on the Web!
StepIntoReading.com
randomhouse.com/kids

Educators and librarians, for a variety of teaching tools, visit us at RHTeachersLibrarians.com

ISBN 978-0-7364-3090-6 (trade) — ISBN 978-0-7364-8143-4 (lib. bdg.)

Printed in the United States of America   10 9

Dear Parent:

Congratulations! Your child is taking the first steps on an exciting journey. The destination? Independent reading!

STEP INTO READING® will help your child get there. The program offers five steps to reading success. Each step includes fun stories and colorful art. There are also Step into Reading Sticker Books, Step into Reading Math Readers, Step into Reading Phonics Readers, Step into Reading Write-In Readers, and Step into Reading Phonics Boxed Sets—a complete literacy program with something for every child.

Learning to Read, Step by Step!

Ready to Read   Preschool–Kindergarten
• big type and easy words • rhyme and rhythm • picture clues
For children who know the alphabet and are eager to begin reading.

Reading with Help   Preschool–Grade 1
• basic vocabulary • short sentences • simple stories
For children who recognize familiar words and sound out new words with help.

Reading on Your Own   Grades 1–3
• engaging characters • easy-to-follow plots • popular topics
For children who are ready to read on their own.

Reading Paragraphs   Grades 2–3
• challenging vocabulary • short paragraphs • exciting stories
For newly independent readers who read simple sentences with confidence.

Ready for Chapters   Grades 2–4
• chapters • longer paragraphs • full-color art
For children who want to take the plunge into chapter books but still like colorful pictures.

STEP INTO READING® is designed to give every child a successful reading experience. The grade levels are only guides. Children can progress through the steps at their own speed, developing confidence in their reading, no matter what their grade.

Remember, a lifetime love of reading starts with a single step!